The Coin
of
Souls

Dragon Riders of Osnen Book 4

RICHARD FIERCE

Dragonfire Press

Cover design by germancreative.

Cover art by Rosauro Ugang

ISBN: 978-1-947329-34-8

CONTENTS

1

It had been two days.

Two days of scouring the city looking for a man I'd only seen once. To say that I was frustrated was a bit of an understatement. And on top of that, Maren had been distracted and detached since we'd left the Citadel. Granted, she was grieving the loss of her dragon, but her downcast appearance was so out of character for her that I was having trouble staying excited about finding the mysterious island the man had mentioned.

"Where did you say this man lived?"

That had been one of only a few things Maren said all day. I looked over my shoulder at her. She was looking down at the cobblestones and absently kicked a small stone. It skittered past me, the sound echoing oddly off the buildings that lined the street around us.

"I think it's up ahead somewhere," I replied. "And I didn't say he lived here. I mean, he might, but I don't know that."

The derelict neighborhood held a gloom that even the sun couldn't penetrate. The air was colder here than on the main streets and a shiver ran down my spine. I rubbed my hands together to warm them, but it didn't help. All of the buildings looked so similar I was afraid that I wouldn't remember where the man had accosted me. I tried to visualize the memory in my mind, but I'd been in a panic about Maren and waylaid by Rory and his men, so the details were foggy. I felt Sion's presence nudging around my mind.

What are you doing? I asked her.

Dragons are better at remembering things, she replied. *If I can see your memory, maybe I can tell you which building it is.*

That seemed logical to me, but I remembered my father telling me that only riders who had been bonded for years could share their memories with their dragon. I supposed it was worth trying, regardless. I went through my memory again.

Can you see it? I asked.

Sion hummed in reply, but I didn't know what that meant. I continued through the fragmented memory and waited for Sion to say something.

I'm sorry, I only got impressions. I didn't see any part of the memory.

It's all right, I replied. *We tried.*

We passed a few more buildings and Sion overwhelmed my mind.

Stop!

I stopped walking. Maren must not have been paying attention, because she ran right into me and almost knocked me over.

"Sorry!" Maren exclaimed.

This is it, Sion said. *On your left. I can feel*

something in your mind attached to this building.

I looked at the place and it did seem faintly familiar.

"It's this one," I said, casting Maren a glance.

The structure was in disrepair like the others, but much worse for wear. The door was open and barely attached to the hinges. Maren shrugged and walked through the open doorway. I followed behind her and looked around the main living area. There wasn't much to see. A broken table and an overturned chair were the only items in the entire place. There wasn't even a bed. The place felt abandoned. I looked through the other rooms for good measure, then came back into the living area.

"There's nothing," I said.

"So I see," Maren replied.

I chewed on my lower lip, thinking. The man might have left the city. If that were the case, I had no idea where he would've gone. I up-righted the chair and offered it to Maren but she declined, so I sat on it and stared at my boots in defeat.

And that's when I saw it.

A piece of parchment was on the floor. There was something drawn on the other side of it. Curiosity made me grab the parchment and I turned it over. It was a hand-drawn map, but I didn't recognize anything on it. There was a tall tower scrawled on it, and next to that was a large 'X' with a circle around it.

"What do you think this is?" I handed the parchment to Maren.

She stared at it for a moment, then said, "A map?"

"Well, yes … but a map of what? Does anything on there seem familiar?"

"No," Maren said without hesitation. She turned it a few different ways and shook her head, handing the map back to me. "I don't know what it's supposed to be a map of."

"Me neither," I said. I heaved a sigh and stood up, then folded the parchment and put it into my coin purse. "Now what?"

Maren shrugged again.

"Right. Well, I guess we can go back to the Citadel. Maybe someone there will be able to tell us something helpful about this map."

Maren fell into step beside me after we left the building. The main streets were packed with people and we had to push our way through the crowds. I held onto Maren's hand tightly so we didn't lose each other and we departed the city through the main gates. As much as I didn't want to go back to the Citadel yet, there wasn't much choice in the matter.

Sion was basking in the sun, her wings outstretched. It could have been my imagination, but she suddenly seemed much larger than when I'd first found her. She looked at me and tilted her head curiously.

What do you have? She asked.

What do you mean?

There's magic radiating off your body.

I had no idea what she was talking about.

"Sion says there's magic coming off me," I said to Maren.

"Really? That's odd … wait. Let me see that map again."

What map? Sion asked.

I pulled the parchment out of my coin purse and handed it to Maren.

I found it in the man's house, I replied. *Neither one of us can make out what the location drawn on it is supposed to be.*

Sion hummed in her throat.

That map has magic glowing on it so bright it's like staring up at the sun.

"I don't know how I missed this," Maren said as she examined the map. "There's a powerful enchantment on this parchment, but I've never seen anything like it before. It's almost blinding to look at."

"That's what Sion said."

I was getting excited about the map. It was clearly special in some regard; otherwise, why would it be enchanted?

"Some words are hovering within the spell, but I

don't know the language. This is really interesting," Maren said.

It was good to see her mind occupied with something other than her grief. I watched her eyes move back and forth over the parchment, seeing things that I was unable to. A smile was tugging at the edge of her mouth.

"I wish you could see this magic, Eldwin," Maren said. "It's so beautiful."

Is it possible to see through your eyes? I asked Sion.

Perhaps.

Sion pushed against the bond and I could feel a strange sensation in my cheek that was slowly making its way upward to the corner of my left eye. My eyelid started twitching and for a brief moment, I saw a bright golden light coming off the parchment before the sensation faded. Sion withdrew from my mind and I suddenly felt exhausted as if I hadn't slept for days.

I'm sorry, Sion said. *I'm not sure if I was doing it right, but I felt your strength diminishing so I stopped.*

It's all right. I saw enough to understand Maren's fascination. Do all enchanted items glow like that?

No, Sion replied. *This magic is rare and powerful.*

Can you read the words that Maren mentioned?

No. It's a magical language, but it is of human origin.

I nodded and leaned against Sion's side to rest for a moment. Her body expanded and contracted as she breathed, her bulk pushing me back and forth.

"Are you ready to go?" I asked Maren.

She looked at me, a full smile stretched across her lips. "Sure. I don't know if anyone at the Citadel will be able to help with this, though," she said. "This is sorcery at its best. Riders might gain magical abilities from their dragons, but this is something entirely different."

"What about the sorcerers in your father's court? Would they be able to help?"

"Maybe, but I don't want to take it to them."

"Then I guess we'll figure it out when we get back to the Citadel," I said. I stood up straight and offered her my hand. She took it and held the parchment in her free hand, then started up Sion's shoulder.

A loud roaring noise suddenly filled the air and the parchment began to glow with a green light. Everything around us fractured like a broken mirror and my stomach dropped as if I was falling. I could feel my breakfast threatening to reappear and closed my eyes. It helped. A little. My stomach calmed and I cracked my eyes open. We weren't outside the city anymore.

We were in a forest.

2

"Where are we?"

Maren's voice shattered my surprise and I looked from her to Sion.

"I have no idea. What did you do?" I asked.

"Me? I didn't do anything!" Maren snapped. "It was this map!"

Sion sniffed the air.

This place smells familiar, she said. *I've been here before.*

Is that a good thing? I asked.

I smell dragons.

"Sion says there are dragons nearby," I told Maren. "That should be a good thing."

The trees around us creaked as their tops swayed from the wind. Not far away, I heard leaves crunching. Someone was approaching. I put my hand on the hilt of my blade, not sure what to expect.

A Terranese man came into view. He was wearing heavy armor and paused when he saw us.

"Hail!" I called out and raised a hand.

"Why do you trespass here?" He replied. "This place is off-limits to everyone outside the school."

"I'm afraid we don't know where we are," I

said. "What school are you talking about?"

The man suddenly seemed to realize that I wasn't alone. He leaned to the side, peering at Sion.

"Are you riders?" He asked.

"Yes," I answered.

"Forgive me. I didn't know. Are you here to see Master Katori?"

Maren and I looked at each other.

"This map brought us all the way to the coast?" Maren whispered incredulously.

"That's what it sounds like. Maybe Katori knows something about this map or the island. It doesn't hurt to ask." I turned my attention back to the man. "Yes, we would like to see Master Katori."

"I will escort you," the man said.

Maren and I followed him out of the woods while Sion launched herself into the air and disappeared above the canopy.

"When you said the enchantment was powerful, I didn't know you meant it could teleport us a few hundred miles away."

"I wouldn't have guessed that it could, but the magic was like nothing else I've ever encountered."

The Terranese man led us around to the front of the school and the guards let us in without question. Some of the buildings were damaged and people were working on repairing them. I marveled again at the beauty of the foreign architecture and was disappointed to see that they had been damaged.

"Please, wait here. I will inform the master that you're here."

"Thank you," I said. The man went into the school and I looked around the courtyard. Most of the debris had been swept into small piles out of the main walkways, but there were a few large pieces of wood still obstructing the area.

Where are you? I asked Sion, looking up at the sky.

The stables, she replied. *They're feeding me.* She hummed contentedly through the bond.

I smiled and turned around when I heard footsteps. It was the man from the woods. He motioned us to follow him and we went inside the school. I remembered how odd everything had seemed to me when we first came to the school. The difference in cultures was staggering, yet we were all alike in respect to the bonds with our dragons.

The thin paper wall that also acted as a door was partially open and I could see Katori sitting cross-legged on the floor. The man cleared his throat and Katori looked up. She smiled when she saw us and rose to her feet.

"Greetings," Katori said. "Please, come in and have a seat."

Maren and I stepped into the room and removed our boots, then sat on the pillows that rested in front of the small table in the center of the room.

"Would you like some tea?"

"No, thank you," I said.

"I'll take some," Maren replied.

"Very well." Katori lifted the teapot from the table and poured two cups, keeping one for herself. She slid the other cup across the table and Maren picked it up and took a sip.

"What brings you out here?" Katori asked. "Is something wrong?"

"No, everything is fine," I said. "As for what brought us here, that's a bit of a story."

"Indulge my curiosity," Katori replied, smiling.

"I'll let Maren explain since she's familiar with magic."

"We found a map that had a powerful enchantment on it. That enchantment was triggered somehow and we found ourselves in the woods beside your school."

"Interesting, but not impossible. Teleportation spells require a large amount of magic, but they are less accurate the further away the location is."

"We were outside Tiradale," Maren replied.

Katori's eyes widened briefly. "Tiradale? That's hundreds of miles away."

"You can imagine our surprise," I said with a laugh.

"A spell that teleports that far of a distance would require a vast amount of magic, greater than any spell I'm aware of."

"That's what I told Eldwin," Maren said. "The enchantment glowed so brightly it was blinding."

"Where did you find this map?" Katori asked.

Maren looked at me.

"I met a man in Tiradale that told me about a place where souls go when they are between this world and the spiritual one," I said. "I didn't believe him at first, but the more I thought about it, the more curious I got."

Katori tilted her head to the side. "What would be the purpose of finding such a place?" She asked.

"To find my father."

"To what end? If he is dead …" Katori trailed off. I knew where she was going with her logic.

"The man also mentioned if you have the payment that the helmsman requires, he will take you to the island and you can bring someone back."

"That sounds like necromancy," Katori said. "Consider what the Necromancer did. How would it be any different?"

"I wouldn't enslave my father," I retorted. "I just want him back."

"I understand," Katori said. "I do, but no good can come of it."

"None of that matters if we can't find the place," Maren said. She held up the map. "Do you recognize anything on here?"

Katori took the map and stared at it for a moment, then nodded her head.

"I've never been there, but I know of the place. There are many tales of people seeing strange things, but nothing has ever been confirmed."

"Great," I said. "I thought we were finally making progress."

"I may not have been there, but I know someone who has," Katori replied. "He even claims to have seen a ghost. If anyone might be able to help you, it would be him."

"You'll help us, then?" I asked.

"In a way, yes. I will not go with you, nor will I provide any riders, but I will send a guide to go with you. I don't agree with your quest to bring a spirit back to the world of the living, but I don't believe that this island exists. There are known dangers in this area, so I will tell you to use caution."

"Sion is here with us, and she's coming on this journey," I said.

"That eases my mind, though it would be wise to have your dragon change shapes. She's not as large as other dragons, but getting to this place—" Katori pressed a finger on the map, "—is difficult."

"I don't understand," I said. I glanced at Maren, but she shrugged. "What do you mean change shapes?"

Katori frowned. "Did your Curates not teach you this?"

"Well, I'm technically not part of the school," I said.

"I've not heard anything about this," Maren said. "Though it may be something that hasn't been covered yet."

"I will attempt to explain it, but if you aren't aware of your dragon's ability, I'll have to provide you with something else. Magic can do many things, and dragons are more connected to the flow of magic than any other creature. One thing they can do is shapeshift into something else."

"Like what?" I asked.

"Anything, if their will is strong enough. My dragon can take the shape of a deer."

"How is that possible? They are massive in size, so where does all of that size go?" It didn't make sense to me.

"Dragons can shift their mass into the unseen realm. I do not know how they can perform this trick. All I know is that it can be done."

Sion? Are you hearing this?

I was not aware of this ability, Sion replied. *It is amusing to consider the forms I could take.*

"You said you would have to give me something else?" I asked.

"Yes. It is a piece of jewelry from ancient times. I would hesitate to give it to you if I didn't know your heart. It's an enchanted collar that forces a dragon to take a human form. They were once used for nefarious purposes, but the Conclave enacted rules against using such things. Most of the collars were destroyed, but there are a few that remain."

"And you have one?" I asked.

Katori nodded. "My master would have destroyed it when he learned that it was here in the school, but the knowledge of unweaving ancient magic has been lost for many years. I will give it to you on the condition that you never use it against your dragon's will."

"I would never do that," I said.

"Swear it," Katori demanded.

"I promise."

Katori seemed satisfied with my oath. "Good. Come, let us see how your dragon looks as a human."

3

The collar was a simple design. It was made of gold and lined on the top with several small emeralds that glowed eerily.

"It is safe to use," Katori said. The unease must have been obvious on my face.

"And you are sure it still works?" Maren asked.

"As sure as one can be, considering how long it's been since its last use. My master used it to show me how a dragon transforms many years ago. No one else has used it."

We were outside the protective walls of the school, standing in the field where enemies had once stood not long ago. Sion was staring at us curiously.

If it hurts at all, tell me. I'll take it off immediately.

I will, she confirmed.

I unclasped the collar and Sion lowered her head. Surprisingly, the collar was fairly light for its size. I suspected magic had something to do with that. The collar opened wide, easily able to fit the neck of a dragon three times bigger than Sion. It slid around her neck and I closed the clasp.

At first, nothing happened. Then slowly the emeralds began to glow brighter. Sion snaked her head to the left, then to the right, then back to the left.

Does it hurt? I asked.

No.

That had been my biggest fear of using the collar. Since she wasn't in pain, that eased my nerves.

It tickles more than anything.

The idea that a dragon could be ticklish seemed absurd, but I didn't question her. She made a chortling noise in her throat that made me laugh. I could feel her mirth flowing through the bond, which made her laugh even more infectious.

"Is it just me, or is she shrinking in size?"

Maren's question made me focus on Sion rather than her laughter and I realized Sion was indeed getting smaller. Her bulk continued to diminish until she was roughly the same height as Maren. As if that wasn't impressive enough, her scales began to smear and fade altogether. It reminded me of a potter modeling clay.

Tan flesh replaced her red hue and her body started to look human. In the span of a few heartbeats, Sion no longer resembled a dragon at all. Standing before me was a beautiful woman with dazzling red hair, brighter and more voluminous than Maren's. And then I realized that she was naked.

Katori stepped past me and handed some clothes to Sion. Sion accepted them slowly as if learning with each passing second how to use her new body.

How do you feel? I asked.

Different ... strange, even.

Is it bad? Do you want me to remove the collar?

No, I am fine.

I averted my eyes as she got dressed and could feel her mind probing mine.

Your memories help me learn, she said. *This form is strange, yet it feels somewhat familiar with your recollections.*

I will help however I can, I replied. *Can you speak with your mouth?*

Sion ran her hands over the material of her shirt and looked at me. Her lips parted and she attempted to speak, but it was barely above a whisper and her speech was full of stutters.

"Don't press yourself too much," I told her aloud. "We don't know much about this magic or its limits, and I'd rather you not hurt yourself somehow."

Fair enough, she said.

"Your dragon is beautiful," Maren complimented.

"I agree," Katori said. "Your guide will be ready shortly ... unless you would like to spend the night at the school and leave in the morning?"

"No, but thank you for your hospitality. I'm eager to be going." I looked at Maren questioningly to see if she agreed and she nodded.

"Yes, so am I. Thank you for this gift," Maren said. "I hope that the collar will serve us well."

Katori offered a low bow. "You both saved my school and my students. Offering my assistance is the least I can do."

I stayed close to Sion while Maren and Katori went back inside the school. Sion was a powerful dragon, but I didn't know how much the collar would hinder her abilities. That would pose a problem, especially if we encountered danger.

Can you breathe fire? I asked.

Sion turned away from me and I waited expectantly for her fire to fill the sky. A few moments later, when that didn't happen, Sion turned back to face me.

The magic keeps my fire from igniting, she said. *It's trapped behind a barrier.*

That's not good. Anything else you notice?

Sion hummed as she contemplated the question.

No, nothing else.

Only time will tell, I said. *Hopefully, that's the only problem.*

We took a walk around the school, exploring the area and enjoying the silence. I wasn't sure where this journey would take us, but I imagined it couldn't be worse than what we'd already been through with the Necromancer and the False King.

Our exploration took us around the entire school and when we ended up back at the gates, Maren was waiting for us.

"Having fun?" She asked, smiling. It was good to see her in better spirits.

"Just walking around," I replied. "I figured it would be good for Sion to get accustomed to her new body before we head out."

"That's a good idea," Maren said.

"Those are the only kind I have," I replied, quoting Maren.

"Very funny, Eldwin, but you know *I* came up with that. You'll need to get your own saying."

I shrugged and laughed. "All right, but don't get jealous when it's better than yours."

Maren was about to offer another quip when an older Terranese man joined us.

"Greetings," the man said. "I am Nojira. Master Katori has asked me to lead you down to the coast."

Maren and I offered a bow.

"Thank you for agreeing to take us," I said. "The area is unfamiliar to us, and we'd rather not get lost."

Nojira smiled, revealing a few missing teeth. I guessed he was in his late fifties or early sixties. His hair was short and white, and he had a long mustache that twisted up at the ends.

"I'm Eldwin and this is Maren."

Should I give him your real name? I asked Sion.

That is agreeable to me.

"And this is Sion," I said, motioning to her.

"It is an honor," Nojira said.

"Do you need to gather any supplies?" I asked.

"No. I don't plan on staying after dark."

That remark gave me pause. "Why not?"

Nojira seemed embarrassed. "I apologize if I seem superstitious, but after what I saw out there, I've made it a rule to be back indoors by nightfall."

"What did you see?" Maren asked.

"It's what I *thought* I saw," Nojira clarified. "I thought I saw ghosts riding across the water in a boat. It was foggy that night, so I have convinced myself that it was simply my imagination."

"Then why don't you stay out after dark?" I asked.

"You don't tempt fate," Nojira said.

I wasn't quite sure what he meant by that, but I didn't press him further.

"If you are ready, we should be going. I'd like to get you there before I have to turn back."

"Lead the way," Maren said.

We headed south, away from the school and toward the coast. Nojira said it was only a few miles, but it was a long trek since the terrain was rough and uneven. Jagged rocks littered the ground and the land curved up and down randomly. We stopped twice to take a break and drink some water, but Nojira kept us moving at a quick pace. Despite his age, he hadn't broken a sweat or complained.

"This place was once ravaged by a volcano," Nojira said. "At least, that's what my grandfather told me. He was a boy when it happened. Everything shook and the waves of the sea were so large they crawled further up the shore than anyone had ever seen."

"That's hard to imagine," I said, wiping sweat from my forehead. "Mainly because I've never been on a boat or seen a storm over the water."

Nojira cackled. "Stay around here long enough and you'll see stranger things than that," he said.

I wasn't so sure that he had fully convinced himself that he'd been seeing things.

Neither am I, Sion said. *I can smell his fear. It grows thicker the closer we get.*

Do you sense anything else? Is there anything about this area that seems odd?

There is one thing, she answered hesitantly.

What is it? I put my hand on the hilt of my sword and glanced around.

It's a song. I can't make out the words, but it is full of sadness.

I listened intently and didn't hear anything unusual, but I kept my guard up anyway. Eventually, the sound of crashing waves reached my ears. When we topped a hill, I saw the source. A long beach stretched as far as I could see. Stretched further still was the sea.

"The Wasted Deep," Nojira said.

"What's what?" Maren asked.

"It's what we call this place. The actual name is the Sea of Colisle. I'm afraid it took us longer to get here than I anticipated, so I must be going back now. May I see your map?"

Maren offered it to Nojira and he held it up for us to see.

"This rock is what you see there," he said, pointing to a large boulder that rested on the beach. "You'll follow the beach past it for a short distance, and then you will find a cove. That is the place you seek."

"Thank you," I said. "Is there anything else we should know?"

"Only one thing," Nojira said.

"What's that?" Maren asked.

Nojira handed the map back to her and his face grew serious.

"You should never have come here."

4

Nojira's words bothered me long after he'd left. They hovered at the back of my mind like an annoying insect as I helped Maren build a fire and prepare to relax for the night. The constant sound of the waves was soothing and after a while, I stopped worrying.

Sion was walking near the water, just out of reach of the waves. It was odd seeing her as a human. I wondered how she would sleep. On the ground like Maren and me? Or perhaps curled up in a ball like she normally slept as a dragon?

"What are you thinking about?" Maren asked as she sat beside me in the sand.

"Sion," I replied.

Maren gave me a curious glance.

"You're not jealous, are you?" I joked.

"No …"

I looked at her and chuckled.

"Well, maybe a little," she admitted. "I mean, she's beautiful as a human."

"True, but she's a dragon. There's nothing to be jealous of."

"Why do you suppose those collars were invented?" Maren asked.

"Katori said it was to enslave dragons. I'm sure people wanted to have control over them. They're probably the most powerful creatures in existence."

"People always have nefarious reasons for creating things like that. I'm glad that the Conclave ended up banning them."

"So am I," I replied.

"I wonder what's going to happen now that the Conclave is gone," Maren said.

"I heard Anesko talking about that. The masters of the schools are discussing changes to the way things have been. I don't think anything has been decided, though."

We remained silent for a moment before Maren got up and retrieved some bread from her pack. She tore the loaf down the center and handed me half.

"I'll take first watch," I offered. I was tired, but I figured Maren would want to rest.

"No, I will," she said. "You can take the second shift."

"What about Sion?" I asked. "Should we let her stand guard also?"

Maren scrunched her face in thought and shook her head. "No. We still don't know her limitations, so I think it's best we don't test her right now."

"That's what I was thinking, too."

After the sun had set, I added more wood to the fire and laid on the ground. It wasn't very comfortable, but I was hoping it would be the only night we had to sleep on the beach. I already felt grimy from the walk, and the sand wasn't helping at all. I drifted off to sleep, content and warm.

I dreamed I was on a boat, the waves rocking me back and forth. Something seemed off about the movement, and I woke up. Through bleary eyes, I saw Maren a few inches from my face.

"It's your turn," she said.

I sat up and stretched. My neck was sore so I figured I must have been sleeping in an awkward position. I got to my feet and walked around the fire a few times, forcing myself to wake up. By the time I was fully awake, Maren was sound asleep in the spot I had been. Sion was also asleep a few feet away. Her body moved up and down with her breathing, a rhythmic pattern that made me wish I was still asleep.

The sound of the waves lapping at the shore drew my attention and I wandered down to the water. I stripped my boots off and let the cool water wash over my feet. A dense fog had rolled into the area, hindering visibility. I faintly heard a chorus of voices singing a melancholy song. The words were elusive, but they invoked powerful images of loss. Souls lost to disease, war, and accidents – all of them begging for guidance.

One moment I was standing there listening to the song, and the next I was lying next to Maren. I blinked lazily, trying to remember how I had gotten there when I noticed someone standing by the fire. As my sleepiness faded, I noticed the figure was a man. I reached for my sword, but it wasn't at my waist. I had no idea where it was.

"What are you doing?" I demanded, rising to my feet.

The figure turned toward me and I saw it was an elderly man. His limbs were so thin and frail-looking, it seemed a miracle he could even stand on his own two legs. A scraggly gray beard hung from his chin and two bushy eyebrows stood in stark contrast to his bald head. He wasn't wearing a shirt and judging by his skinny appearance, he hadn't eaten in weeks.

"I'm getting warm," he replied in a raspy voice.

The sound grated on my nerves. The old man dug his toes into the sand and I realized he didn't have shoes on. The only thing he wore was a tattered pair of pants that had more patches than I'd ever seen.

"Who are you?" I asked, confused. Where had he come from?

"Just a simple man," he replied.

"I mean, what's your name?"

"My name?" The man rubbed his hands together near the fire. "No one has asked for my name in a long time. I don't suppose I remember it. People just call me the ferryman."

The ferryman? Realization dawned on me. This was the helmsman, the person that crazy man from Tiradale had mentioned.

"You ferry people from here to the island, right?"

The man cleared his throat several times and spat into the fire. It sizzled in response.

"People? No, I don't ferry people. Not recently, anyway. I ferry waywards across the sea."

"What's a wayward?" I asked.

"A lost soul. They don't know where to go when they break free of their body, so I take them across the sea and drop them off."

The more the man talked, the less his voice irritated me. I could still hear the song echoing off the water, but it was weaker than before. I stared out at the dark surface of the water, but I saw nothing except a small boat.

A boat.

"You hear it, don't you?" The ferryman asked.

"Hear what?"

"The song," he replied. "I used to find it sad, but now? Now it feels like home."

"You said you haven't taken anyone to the island recently?"

"I've taken plenty of waywards, but I haven't taken a mortal in a long while."

"The last person you took there … who was he looking for?" I asked.

The ferryman reached up and scratched his smooth head. "I don't remember. His wife, I think.

That sounds right."

"How long ago was that?"

"You ask a lot of questions."

"I'm sorry," I said. "There's a lot I don't know."

"Life is full of mysteries," the ferryman replied.

"Indeed, it is. I'm looking for someone that I think is on the island. Can you take me there?"

"I can take you," he said. "If you've got the payment I seek."

"How much? I have a bag full of gold coins from Osnen."

"I don't take gold," the ferryman said, spitting into the fire again. "I only take silver."

I reached into my coin purse and felt around for the silver coin I'd received during my test. It was larger than the gold coins and I pulled it out and held it up for his inspection.

"Will this work?"

The ferryman whistled in admiration and reached for the coin. I handed it over willingly and watched as he put part of the coin in his mouth and bit down on it.

"I haven't seen one of these in years," he said. "And it's genuine. You must have some generous friends."

I shrugged in response. "What about my friends? Does the payment cover them, too?"

The ferryman looked at Maren and shook his head. "I'm afraid not. One traveler per coin." His left eye twitched when he glanced at Sion. "I'll wave the fee for her," he said, nodding in Sion's direction. "Dragons don't count as mortals."

"How did you know she's a dragon?" I blurted out.

"When you've been around as long as I have, nothing escapes your notice."

That didn't explain *how* he knew, but I didn't want to press him. He'd agreed to take me to the island, and that was all that mattered.

"When do we leave?" I asked.

"Soon," the ferryman replied. "I'm waiting on a few more waywards."

I knelt beside Maren and shook her gently. She groaned and cracked her eyes open.

"It's not daylight yet," she huffed. "It's still your shift."

"The ferryman is here," I whispered.

She bolted up suddenly and looked around. The ferryman offered her a toothy grin.

"I need to go to the island," she said. "I have money."

"He doesn't take normal money," I replied. "Do you remember the coin I got from my test? That's the only thing he accepts."

"You don't take anything else?" Maren asked,

the desperation in her voice clawing at my heart.

"I'm afraid not," the ferryman said.

"Nothing at all?"

He opened his mouth as if to reiterate his reply, then paused. A grin spread across his lips.

"Actually, there is something I'll consider."

"What is it?" Maren asked.

"A boon. I'll tell you what it is when the time comes."

I didn't know why, but I didn't like the way he said that.

"Deal," Maren said before I could object.

"Excellent! Climb onto my humble vessel and let us depart for the Island of Lost Souls."

5

As we sailed across the Sea of Colisle, it felt more like we were gliding among the clouds than over water. The thick fog obscured everything beyond a few feet, yet the ferryman guided the boat with a practiced ease. A small lantern hung from a pole at the front of the vessel. It created an interesting orange glow but it did little to pierce the haze.

It was hard to discern the passage of time. When I assumed we were halfway across, I heard the mournful song again. The volume was louder and filled the air all around us. I peered over the side of the boat, thinking that whoever was singing had to be nearby. The ferryman gave me a hard look and I backed away.

"Where is that song coming from?" I asked.

"It's hard to tell," the ferryman answered. "Sirens are tricky creatures. It sounds like they are close, but they may be a fair distance from us."

"What's a siren?"

"So many questions," the ferryman rasped in exasperation.

"Sorry," I muttered.

"Sirens are a myth," Maren said. "Legends say that they are like mermaids, but they lure men into the water to murder them."

"They are no myth," the ferryman said. "Trust me."

Maren rolled her eyes and I hid my smile. Sion was standing at the prow of the boat and the glow from the lantern made her look like she had an eerie aura shining around her. She hadn't spoken since we'd boarded the boat.

Is everything all right? I asked her.

Yes. I'm watching the sirens.

I gave Maren a concerned look.

They're real?

They are as visible as you and me, but not as visible as the company we have on the boat.

Despite the fact that I knew there was only four people on the boat, I looked around anyway. A chill ran down my spine and my skin rose with goosebumps.

What company?

I felt Sion moving around in my mind much like when she had showed me the enchantment on the map. My vision blurred momentarily, and then I saw a group of ghostly figures all around us. Sion was able to hold her focus longer this time and I was able to see the details of some of the apparitions.

To my right, there was a Terranese man. He was fully armored and appeared to have been in a battle. Standing beside the ferryman was a figure I had never seen before. He was tall and thin, with pale skin and light blond hair. His most striking feature was his pointed ears. Whatever he was, he wasn't human.

A thick but diminutive woman stood beside Sion at the prow, though she wasn't tall enough to see over the side. I knew she was a female because of her body type, but she wore a long beard that reminded me of Nojira. There were a few other spirits as well, but Sion released my mind and they faded from sight. The ferryman had said that he transported lost souls, but I thought he was just spinning me a tale. It seemed there was more truth to his claim than I had first thought.

"Can you see the waywards?" I asked the ferryman.

"I can."

"The tall one with the pointed ears … what is he?"

The ferryman smirked. "You've never seen an elf before?"

"Never," I confirmed, shaking my head. "What about the one at the front, next to Sion?"

Dwarf.

"A dwarf."

Sion and the ferryman spoke at the same time.

How do you know what she is? I asked.

She told me. Her name is Thegul Alebane.

That's a weird name, I replied.

That's amusing. She said the same thing about yours.

"Can you see them?" I asked Maren.

"Somewhat," she replied. "I can see faint outlines, enough to know that something is there, but magic has its limits."

"What do the waywards do when they get to the island?" I asked the ferryman.

"I wouldn't know," he said. "They can't leave, though. Not unless a mortal brings them back or their purpose is fulfilled on the island."

So, the man from Tiradale *wasn't* crazy. At least, not entirely. That meant that if my father was on the island, it was possible for me to bring him back. Determination filled my mind. I was sure I was going to see him again.

"You said you've never been on the island yourself?" I asked.

"Never," the ferryman confirmed.

"Do you know if it's dangerous?"

A smile tugged at the old man's lips. "There is danger in everything."

I supposed he was right, but that didn't answer my question. I sat beside Maren and listened to the song of the sirens, wondering what they looked like.

Hideous, Sion answered my thought. *Do you want to see?*

No, I answered after a brief pause. I was

curious, but if Sion thought they were ugly, I wasn't so sure I wanted that image burned into my memory. I closed my eyes and leaned my head against Maren's shoulder. I had either dozed off or lost track of time, but the boat jarred to a stop and I latched onto Maren's arm to keep from falling forward. She shook her head but smiled at me.

"We're here," the ferryman announced.

I rose to my feet and helped Maren up, then hauled myself over the edge of the boat and onto the beach. The fog was still thick, but I was able to see a little better than when we were on the water. Sion and Maren joined me and I looked at the ferryman.

"What's the best way to find someone?" I asked.

"How should I know? I told you I've never been on the island before."

"Right. Well, then."

"How long do you stay here before you go back?" Maren asked.

"Until I hear the call of the next group of waywards. It could be a few minutes or a few hours. There's no way to know."

"If we come back and you aren't here, is there a way to call for you or do we just wait until you come back?"

"You'll have to wait on me."

"Fair enough," I said. "See you soon."

I turned toward the island and headed up the

beach, taking the lead. Maren followed behind me and Sion took up the rear. Sand crunched beneath my boots as I walked, but there weren't any other sounds. Not even birds cried overhead. I assumed that there probably weren't many souls here and that it should be relatively easy to find my father.

The fog ended abruptly like a curtain suddenly pulled away. In the distance, a black mountain rose from the ground and a massive cloud of steam shrouded its top. Where the sand of the beach ended, thick green grass took its place. The change was so sudden, I guessed that someone must have created this place.

"This place is covered with ancient magic," Maren said, confirming my suspicions.

It's everywhere, Sion added. *The magic is woven into the entire fabric of the island.*

Can you sense any souls nearby?

No. There are many here, but none close. We need to go further in that direction.

Sion pointed with her human hand toward the mountain. I nodded and started walking. After a few minutes, I became aware of the souls that had been on the boat with us. They were visible now, but they had a faint glowing outline that left no doubt that they weren't mortals.

"Bah, this is torture, I tell you," the dwarven woman muttered.

I glanced to my left and saw the elf walking beside me.

"Greetings," he said. "I am Galaeron."

"I'm Eldwin," I replied, feeling a little odd about speaking with a spirit.

"Who are you looking for?" Galaeron asked.

"My father," I answered.

"I'm sorry to hear of your loss."

I would have explained to the elf that I'd lost my father long ago, but the whole thing was so complicated that I didn't bother.

"How did you die?" As soon as I asked, I realized that it could be considered rude to ask. If it was, the elf didn't seem to mind.

"I was poisoned," Galaeron said.

"That's terrible," Maren chimed in.

"Indeed, yet it is the way of things where I'm from."

Galaeron looked at Sion curiously. "Where did you get a dragon servant?" He asked.

"She's not a servant," I replied. "We are bonded. I am her rider."

"That's intriguing. Dragons are servants in my land."

"Not in ours," Maren said.

The more about the world I learned, the less I seemed to like it. If it wasn't for Katori's collar, the idea that dragons could be servants would have been ludicrous.

"It was nice meeting you," I told Galaeron, "but I'm short on time. I hope you find a way to get off the island."

Galaeron offered a slight bow of his head and I picked up the pace, leaving the ghosts behind. As we continued closer to the mountain, I noticed that tremors shook the ground every so often.

"What do you suppose is causing that shaking?" I asked.

"I was wondering that myself," Maren replied. "I'm not sure."

The mountain, Sion said. *It's full of fire and brimstone. I can smell it.*

"That's a volcano?" I asked aloud.

Yes. We should hurry and get off this island.

Why?

I can feel the tension in the ground. It won't be long before it erupts.

6

We made good time to the base of the mountain. I attributed the threat of death by volcano as the main reason for our brisk pace, and neither Maren nor Sion complained. As we trekked along the grassy plains, the sound of battle filled the air. Other than the noise, there was nothing else to indicate fighting. The sky was overcast with gray clouds, but there was no threat of rain and no smoke.

I drew my blade, though I wasn't sure what good it would do against ghosts. The distance between us and the battle closed and my eyes widened in disbelief. Apparitions materialized and faded from view everywhere, the souls of various races warring against one another in the largest battle I'd ever seen.

"What's happening?" I muttered aloud.

"The battle for Eternal Glory," a voice answered from beside me.

I glanced over to see Galaeron. The elf kept his eyes on the battle.

"They war without end with the expectant hope that one day they will rise from the island into the realm of their chosen god."

"Will you join in the battle also?" I asked.

"No," Galaeron replied. "My people do not

believe in such fairy tales."

I couldn't help but wonder if my father was in the battle, but there were so many ghosts it was impossible to tell. None of the souls died as they were struck with blows that would have been mortal wounds for someone alive. They merely disappeared momentarily, then returned and continued fighting as if nothing had happened.

We watched in silence for a while, entranced by the sight. I scanned the area looking for anyone that resembled my father, but there was nothing but chaos. I did see something else, though. Amidst the grass, a path of white stones stuck out. It wound its way up the side of the mountain. I followed it with my eyes, but it continued so high that it faded from sight.

"I wonder what that is," I said, nudging Maren and pointing to the path.

"There's only one way to find out," she replied.

The magic is concentrated there, Sion said. *It flows from the mountain like a raging river. It calls to me, but ...*

But what? I asked.

There isn't much time.

For a moment, I considered turning back and fleeing the island. Our lives weren't worth the risk of dying in a rain of fire, but the stubborn part of me refused to miss the chance of bringing my father back. I doubted the ferryman would give me my coin back, and as far as I knew, there was no other way to get here.

I'll hurry. If we don't find him quickly, we'll get off the island. I would never let anything happen to you, I told Sion. Whether or not she believed me, I couldn't tell. Her thoughts had been guarded ever since we got on the island. She trusted me, and that was enough to force me to think of her and Maren more than my own selfish quest.

"You can wait here if you want," I said. "I don't expect either of you to follow me."

Our bond is strongest when we are together, Sion said.

"I'm not letting you see what's up there without me," Maren huffed.

"Fine," I replied and sheathed my blade.

There wasn't a way to go around the ghosts to get to the path, so that left only one option. We had to go *through* them. My only concern with that was whether or not souls had the ability to enter mortal bodies. I didn't think that was possible considering a living person had their own soul, but it was an unknown risk.

"We're going to run through that mess without stopping. On my count," I said. "One, two—"

"Three!" Maren shouted as she sprinted ahead.

Sion and I ran after her. The apparitions swirled around us, swinging weapons that passed through us but struck their ghostly enemies. I didn't feel any of it, but I still flinched when the various blades came at me. We crossed through the army of ghosts and came out on the other side. The stones of the path were made of white marble with striations of silver that crisscrossed their surface.

"This reminds me of the palace," Maren said. "My great grandfather had statues carved of the same stone."

I nodded at her, but my attention was being pulled to the path. A faint humming sound was coming from it. I knelt and lowered my head close to one of the stones and the humming intensified.

"Can you hear that?" I asked.

"Can you?" Maren replied, surprised.

"Yes. Why?"

"That's the sound of magic. It's extremely powerful right here. Maybe that's why you can hear it."

I stood up and shrugged. "Maybe." I was about to step onto the path when a deep voice grumbled, "Halt."

A dwarf, this one a male, was walking toward us. His feet seemed to hover above the stones of the path as he approached.

"This path is not for the living," he said, his voice somber. "Only wayward souls may continue."

"Why aren't the living allowed on it?" I asked.

"The Path of Sacrifice asks for much and gives little. Many who've come this way have perished for lack of strength."

"I'm strong enough," I replied stubbornly.

"You may be," the dwarf said. "Each plateau you will find someone dear to you that will ask you to give up something. If you accept their request, you will be tested and given a key if you pass the test. The key will allow you to go to the next plateau."

"And if I fail?" I asked.

"Then you will perish, and your soul will be trapped here for eternity."

"I accept the consequences," I said.

Is that wise? Sion asked.

I hope so, I told her.

The dwarf stared at me with large eyes. Where the color of his pupils should have been, there was only blackness. He finally lowered his head and stretched out his arm.

"Go," he bade sadly.

I frowned as doubt filled me, but I reminded myself that I hadn't come this far for nothing. I looked from Sion to Maren, then stepped onto the path. Nothing happened. Relief washed over me and I continued along the stones.

"He was just being dramatic, I suppose," I said.

"Maybe," Maren replied. "There is something odd about these stones, though. And I'm not sure I like it."

We walked for a few hundred feet and there was

no one in sight. The mountain slowly sloped upward, and the stones seemed to hum louder the further we traveled. My doubt and uneasiness faded and I felt confident my decision had been a good one.

"Well, there doesn't appear to be any ghosts here," I said, glancing around.

Except for that one, Sion replied.

I looked ahead and froze in place. It was my mother. My throat constricted and tears welled in my eyes, blurring my vision. I blinked rapidly and rushed forward to embrace her, but when I touched her, my hands passed through her incorporeal form.

"Eldwin, my son. How I long to hold you once more." Her words almost broke me.

"Mother, I miss you so much! Why are you here? How are you a lost soul?"

"I'm not sure," she answered. "The gods have plans that we do not understand, but I feel that my time here grows short. Perhaps your arrival is related to that feeling."

"Whatever I can do to help you be free of the island, tell me. I will do it."

"I need you to give me your boots," she said.

"My boots?" The request was an odd one, but if she needed them, then I would willingly give them to her.

"Yes. Please take them off and place them on the ground."

I did as she asked, and her eyes turned completely white. She seemed to be overtaken by some unseen force. Her form trembled.

The magic is funneling into her body, Sion said.

When my mother spoke again, it was an otherworldly sound.

"Behold, a portal is opened. Step inside and find the golden key."

The air rippled beside her and I looked at Sion and Maren. "Wish me luck," I said, then hurried through the portal before they could argue. Everything around me shifted awkwardly and I felt like I was going to be sick. A wave of heat washed over me and the landscape settled into place. The ground was black, and steam rose from cracks that spiderwebbed across the dark surface.

My feet grew uncomfortably warm and as I surveyed my surroundings, I quickly realized the danger of where I was. The ground wasn't black dirt, it was molten rock. A glance into one of the crevices revealed bright glowing lava. Across the river of cooled magma was a marble pedestal, and tall earthen walls rose around me. I wasn't at the bottom of the volcano anymore.

I was inside it.

7

The ground rumbled ominously beneath my bare feet as I made my way carefully across the semi-cooled magma. The heat was still suffocating even though the lava wasn't fresh. I stepped on a soft spot and the blackness gave way. I was able to pull my foot back up before I was burned, but the close call frightened me.

What's happening? Sion asked. *Your fear is overwhelming.*

I'm fine, I said. *This place is grueling. Maybe I made a mistake in coming here.*

We never know the risks until we go where we've never been. Perhaps we will yet find your father.

If not, I could take my mother back, I said.

You could.

I needed to focus, so I closed the bond and gritted my teeth against the burning sensation that spread across my feet. I did a quick mental countdown and then sprinted the rest of the way to the pedestal. It was roughly four feet in height and was made of the same marble as the stones from the path. Laying atop its surface was a golden key. I grabbed it and waited to be transported back to the path, but nothing happened.

Something wasn't right. I had retrieved the key,

so why was I still here? I examined the pillar and found a movable panel on the side of it. The panel slid open easily at my touch and I saw a keyhole. I slipped the key inside and turned it the only direction it would go. There was a click and the top of the pillar opened. Inside the hidden compartment was another key. It was almost identical to the other one with the exception that this one had a small green emerald embedded at the top.

It glowed like the emeralds in Sion's collar, prompting me to wonder about the significance. I shrugged and removed the key from the compartment. It was heavier than the first key. The emerald flashed and the pillar faded from sight. The landscape faded as well, leaving me standing on nothing but darkness.

Just as panic started to grip me, the darkness was replaced by the sight of my mother. She was looking down at me, smiling. She looked just like I remembered her before she got sick. Her long brown hair was straight and reached down past her shoulders and her brown eyes were lively and full of love. I realized I was lying on the ground. Maren's face appeared and she offered me her hand and pulled me onto my feet.

"That was weird and terrifying all at the same time," I said.

"The key," my mother said, her tone somewhat urgent.

I handed it to her, then she turned around and slid it into the empty air and turned it. I glanced at

Maren but she shrugged, just as confused as I was. The key dissipated in a swirl of golden sand and my mother turned back.

"Leave your boots and proceed."

If leaving my boots behind was one of the sacrifices the path wanted, I supposed I could go without them. It was annoying, but I could always get another pair.

"I'll see you again one day," I said.

"Not too soon, I hope," my mother replied. "Go and find peace, my son."

I walked past her and paused. When I turned back to say something more, she was gone. I sighed and continued up the path, Sion and Maren close behind me. I stared down at the stones as I walked, struggling to continue the journey. I didn't like this place. It was confusing, terrifying, and torturous. I wanted to leave, but that would mean I had come here for nothing, that I had endangered Sion and Maren for no reason. I couldn't bear the thought. I—

"Eldwin!"

The voice was familiar. I looked up to see Master Pevus. He was wearing his robes from the school and his face was clear of the worry I constantly saw when he was alive.

"Master Pevus?" I said.

"I see you took my words literally when I said you'd have to find your own dragon," he chuckled.

"I did, though our bond was somewhat of an accident. How did you know she was a dragon?" I asked.

"She's wearing a collar," he answered. "The Citadel has one, but it uses different gems. It hasn't been used in quite some time, of course, but it works the same."

"This one was given to me by the master of the Terranese school," I said. "I had no idea that there was so much in the world I wasn't aware of."

"There's much more than you can fathom," Pevus said. "I lived a long life, and yet now that I am here, I have learned even more. Tell me, Eldwin. Why are you here?"

"I'm looking for my father's soul," I replied.

"Ah, yes. I should have guessed as much. I did find it odd when he turned up here, but he told me of his imprisonment. If I'd have known about the Necromancer, I would like to believe I'd have been able to help."

Pevus looked at Maren. "And why are you not at the Citadel?"

"I'm helping Eldwin," she replied.

"Tell me the truth, princess. You were one of the most rebellious students I've ever had, so I know there's more to the story."

Maren nodded and she was overcome with sadness. "Demris was killed in battle," she said softly. "I was hoping that I might find him here."

"There is something you both seem to be missing," Pevus said, crossing his arms. "The wayward souls here *can* go back to the world of the living, but they are never the same as they were."

"What do you mean?" I asked.

"When a soul is untethered from its body, the connection to who they were is still there, but it's not the same. They retain their memories, but those memories are just fragments of something they don't truly know anymore. What do you think happens to a soul that returns to find they have no physical body anymore?"

That question gave me pause. What *did* happen? And since they didn't have a body, how would they be alive again? That was something I hadn't considered. Now that I thought about it, this journey started to seem like a bigger mistake than I feared.

"I assumed that once they reached the mainland, they would form a new body somehow," Maren said. "Perhaps a magical one."

"Magic can do many great things, but it cannot create life." Master Pevus looked back at me. "If you are intent on this course, you will need to leave your dragon with me. Maren may go with you."

Perhaps this was part of the sacrifice the path required … that I had to give up the hope that I would have my father back. Fine. I would play along.

"I am intent," I said. "Though I cannot force my dragon to do anything."

Will you stay behind? I asked Sion.

I do not want to, but if I must ... I could sense her hesitation.

If it's like the last illusion, I'll be back quickly.

And if it's not? Sion asked.

I didn't answer. "She will stay," I said. "I need to bring you a key, right?"

Master Pevus smiled, but there was no mirth behind it. "Yes. The key will be difficult to obtain. You must be prepared to do whatever it takes to bring it to me."

"I will," I said.

"The path requires much," Pevus warned. "Much more than you are ready to give, I'm sure."

"I'm ready," I said, trying not to let his words bother me visibly.

"Very well."

Master Pevus closed his eyes and whispered something, then looked at me and snapped his fingers. I was jerked backward roughly and I hit the ground. Instead of landing painfully, I was sucked through the ground and found myself in a mirror-like recreation of where I'd just been.

"This is weird," Maren said from beside me. "Was the first one like this?"

"No," I replied. "This one is worse."

We were standing on the path, but the stones were black instead of white. The volcano glittered with thousands of diamonds on its surface. I knelt and tried to pry one loose, but the precious gem didn't budge.

"I'm getting a bad feeling about this place," Maren whispered. "Let's find the key and get out of here."

I stood back up and surveyed the landscape. Unlike the last place, there was nothing in sight. No pillar, nothing.

"I'm not sure where to look," I said. "I suppose we should walk up the path. Maybe the key is up there?"

"That sounds better than standing here," Maren replied. She started up the mountainside at a quick pace. I followed after her and continuously looked around for something, anything at all. It felt like we had walked several miles before the path split in two directions. One continued up the mountain and the other turned right and led into the dark opening of a cave.

Maren went right. I stopped to rest for a moment, but she kept going and disappeared into the cave.

"Maren!" I shouted. "Wait for me!"

I hurried to the cave's entrance and stopped. It was pitch black inside. I listened for sounds of Maren's movements, but there was only silence.

"Maren!"

My voice echoed back at me, eerie and

distorted.

A shadow detached itself from the darkness and walked toward me. I staggered back as it approached. It was a literal shadow shaped like a person, but there were no distinguishing details.

"What are you?" I asked, still backing away.

"I am you," the shadow replied. It was my voice that came from it.

"What do you want?"

The shadow stopped moving and tilted its head to the side. "I want to save Maren."

"Where is she?" I asked.

"She's in there," the shadow said, pointing to the cave. "And she's going to die."

8

As soon as I stepped into the cave's entrance, the darkness faded and I stood before a vast pool of dark water. The surface of the liquid churned oddly as if every drop had a life of its own. Torches lined the walls of the chamber, bathing everything in a lurid orange glow. The shadow that claimed to be me stood at my right. It was like someone had cut out my shape from a black piece of parchment and gave it life. It had no eyes, no mouth, no features at all—yet when it spoke, I heard it clearly.

"We must do something," it said. "One of them will fall into the pit, and you can't save both."

Above the murky water were two cages suspended by chains. Those chains were attached to a pulley system that kept the cages level with one another. A robed figure, a ghost judging by its ethereal outline, stood near a lever that was attached to the pulleys.

As if to demonstrate the predicament Maren was in, the figure pushed the lever forward and Maren's cage slowly lowered while the other cage went higher. The ghost released the lever and the cages settled back into place.

Near the top of the chamber was a ledge that encircled the area. I assumed if one cage went low enough, the other cage would be raised enough to reach the ledge and allow the occupant to get out.

"How do we get over there to control the lever?" I asked.

"You can't," the shadow said. "Those insects will eat you alive."

"Insects?" I looked down at the water and stared intently at the surface. The water wasn't water at all. The pit was filled with thousands of small black insects with glossy shells.

"What are they?" I asked.

"Skin beetles," the shadow replied. "They devour the flesh of living things."

"You aren't a living thing. Why can't you get over there?"

"Wards preventing me from crossing the pit," the shadow said.

I watched the figure near the lever and considered how I might get across. I could possibly scale the wall, but that would take too long. That and if I slipped, I'd be bug food. If I were a sorcerer, I could probably do any number of things to free Maren, which made me wonder why she hadn't used magic to escape. Unfortunately, there didn't seem to be an easy way out of this situation.

"Is one life worth more than another?" The figure's voice echoed off the walls of the cave. "You ponder how to free your friend, but have you considered the stranger?"

I looked at the other cage. The man inside seemed to be alive, though unmoving. He was thin and lanky, but he wasn't starved. It didn't appear that he was a prisoner, which begged the question: who was he? Why was he here? And the figure posed a valid question. Was one life worth more than another? For me, the answer was simple. Yes. Maren was precious to me, but the stranger … well, I knew nothing about him. He was nobody to me.

"Your thoughts betray you here," the figure said.

"You can read my mind?" I asked.

"Not quite. The insects can hear them, and they repeat what they hear. Listen carefully and you might discern their words."

I held my breath and listened. At first, I didn't hear anything other than the sound of their movements. Then slowly bits and pieces started to break away from the noise.

The stranger … nobody …

Their voices were creepy and made my skin crawl.

Blood … we crave blood …

"How do we free Maren?" I asked.

"A choice must be made, a sacrifice given. The path demands it."

"Wait. Are you saying I have to choose between Maren and that person?" I waved a hand toward the stranger's cage.

"Yes," the shadow answered. "He wants you to make a choice."

"I can't do that," I said.

"You must," the figure replied. "Or the path will make the choice for you. And the path chooses the greatest sacrifice."

Dread knotted within my stomach. I had to choose who died?

Choose ... who died ... the insects' voices repeated.

"You are only seeing the choice in a negative light," the figure said. "Instead of thinking that you are condemning someone to die, consider that you are giving someone life."

"I didn't put either of these people in these cages!" I snapped. "Making me choose who dies, or who lives, isn't fair!"

"Life is never fair, nor is it just," the figure replied. "Life simply is."

"I won't choose! I'll just leave this place."

"As I said, the path will choose for you. And you cannot leave until a choice has been made and a sacrifice has been given."

Coming to this island had been a mistake, I decided. Whether I brought my father back, or my mother, didn't matter anymore. Not if this was the cost. I should have heeded the dwarf's warning and never stepped onto the path.

Heeded ... warning ... never ... path ...

"You can't let the regret of your past choices dictate your future ones," the shadow said.

"It's not my choice to make," I replied. "I'm not a god."

"Exactly!" The shadow said excitedly.

I looked at it, confused. With no facial features, it was impossible to read into the shadow's excitement.

"I don't understand. If I'm correct that it's not my choice, then what's the purpose of this?"

The shadow tapped its head. "What indeed?"

I turned my attention to the cages. If it wasn't my choice, then …

"Maren!" I shouted.

She stirred within the cage and turned to face me, her eyes lighting up. "Eldwin!"

It seemed impossible that she hadn't known I was here, but I supposed the magic of the path must have subdued her. That explained why she hadn't tried to escape on her own.

"I need you to answer a question," I said.

"If it will get me out of here, then ask away!"

"Is your life worth more than his?" I asked, nodding toward the other cage.

Maren looked at the man, then back at me. She seemed confused by the question and frowned. "What kind of question is that?"

"The path is asking for a sacrifice. You or him. I can't make that choice."

Realization dawned across Maren's face as she looked down into the pit of insects. The eagerness of the insects reflected in their tone. They began chattering wildly, the logic of their words lost except for one, which they chanted over and over.

Blood, blood, blood.

"I'm sorry for bringing you here," I told Maren. "I just want to leave."

"Don't be sorry," she replied. "I could have stayed at the Citadel. I wanted to come with you."

"I know, but I can't help feeling guilty."

"I'm the one who should feel guilty, Eldwin."

"What do you mean?" I asked.

"I can't let an innocent person die for no reason."

Her words hung in the air, thick and suffocating. I didn't want to accept what she was saying. I couldn't.

"Don't." That was all I could say, but there was a mountain of emotion behind it.

"Lower my cage," Maren said to the robed ghost. "I offer myself as the sacrifice."

"No!" I shouted. "Don't listen to her!"

The ghost didn't pay me any heed. He pushed the lever and Maren's cage began to descend toward the waiting insects. I rushed to the edge of the pit, but the shadow latched onto my arm and kept me from jumping.

"If you go in there, everything you've done for the path will have been in vain," the shadow said.

"I don't care!" I replied. "Maren means more to me than anything. I can't lose her!"

Maren stared at me as the cage lowered slowly yet inexorably toward the deadly insects below. My heart pounded in my chest. There was nothing I could do to stop it. I had never felt more helpless in my entire life.

The bottom of the cage reached the insects and they swarmed up the metal, a wave of black death devouring everything in its path. It seemed like a dream. I told myself that it wasn't real. And I almost believed it.

Until Maren started screaming.

I covered my ears and turned away, unable to bear the sight of her being consumed by the insects. The shadow stood beside me, but nothing about its presence gave me comfort. I frantically tried to reach Sion through the bond, but there was nothing but silence. Something dark and heavy was blocking our bond.

I didn't know how long I stood there before I noticed that Maren's screams had stopped. It could have been minutes, but it felt like days. My mind was numb. Something wet rolled down my cheek. It was probably a tear, but I didn't care if it was something worse. Maren was gone. It was hard to breathe.

"The path has accepted the sacrifice," the ghost

said. "You are to be commended. It wasn't your choice to make, and you knew that."

The ghost's words meant nothing to me. The last thing I remembered before I collapsed to the ground was the ghost's final words.

"The path demands much and gives little in return."

9

When I came back to my senses, I was no longer in the cave.

Master Pevus and Sion stood side by side, staring down at me. Pevus looked troubled at my appearance, but Sion's expression looked like she was worried about me.

What happened? She asked. *Where's Maren?*

I bit my lip and shook my head and I almost lost it. My eyes welled with tears and my legs started to tremble involuntarily. I clenched my fists and realized something was in my right hand. Spreading my mangled fingers open, I saw a golden key resting in my palm. I stared at it through blurred vision.

"How?" I asked aloud.

Master Pevus stepped closer and gently took the key from my hand. He turned around and stuck the key into the air like my mother had, then turned back to face me.

"I'm sorry," Pevus said quietly. He cleared his throat. "Maren was … well, there are no words that would adequately describe her. I'm sorry," he repeated. "The way forward is open. You may continue the journey."

"I can't," I said. "It was stupid to come here. I don't know what I was thinking." I swallowed hard and tried to fight back the tears, but they flowed freely from my eyes. "I was selfish and it has cost me too much. I can't continue." I sat on the path and wrapped my arms around my knees.

"You are right to grieve," Pevus said. "No one begrudges you that. Yet if you give in now, you've lost more than what you realize."

"It hurts!" I cried out.

"I know. I've felt the sting of loss before, and it is a vicious agony, but you must continue. Your time here is fleeting, Eldwin. You must go."

Pevus knelt in front of me and laid a comforting hand on my shoulder.

"Sion can give you focus if you let her."

"What do you mean?" I asked.

"Dragons can handle emotional trauma more effectively than we can. She can take the burden of your grief so that you can clear your mind. It is only temporary, and when she releases your emotions back to you, it will be overwhelming."

Pevus looked over his shoulder as the ground rumbled. I looked up at the top of the volcano and saw steam and ash erupting into the air.

The pressure of the magic is pushing the mountain to the brink, Sion said. *Please, Eldwin. We must go. Give me your grief if you must, but we need to hurry.*

"How do I give her my emotions?" I asked.

Pevus turned his attention back to me. "When

you speak to her, you envision the bond within your mind. It is the same, but you must force the emotions from your mind. Imagine the grief as something pliable and divert it into the bond."

I closed my eyes and imagined that my grief was a raging river. It flooded my senses and I almost lost myself to the madness that lay under the surface of the tumultuous water. I shaped hills around the river, forcing it to travel toward the bond.

Are you ready? I asked Sion.

Yes.

The river of emotion hit the bond and sizzled like it was hitting open flames. Everything I was feeling drained free and the cloudiness around my thoughts faded. Once the grief was absorbed by Sion, my mind was free. Free of sadness, of doubt. I calmly stood up and hugged Master Pevus. He smelled of old parchment and, oddly, berries.

I released him and continued up the path. Sion walked at my side and I looked over at her to see if she was struggling with my grief. Her face was impassive.

What is it? She asked.

Are you all right?

Yes. I am sad that Maren is gone, but I was not bonded to her. I do not feel pained by it, but I understand why you are affected so.

It was an odd sensation to not feel grief. I

expected it to hit me when Sion said Maren's name, yet there nothing but clarity.

We will complete whatever the path has for us, and then we will leave this accursed place. I never want to see it again.

Sion hummed in agreement.

The path angled upward, getting steeper as we continued. My legs burned with the exertion of the climb, but Sion didn't seem bothered at all. By the time the path leveled out, she was basically pulling me along. I stopped to catch my breath and give my muscles a break. The ground was rumbling more consistently now.

I hope this is almost over, I said.

The magic is pooling ahead and I do not see any more of it beyond. I think we are near the end.

Good.

There was tension building in my neck, so I stretched my head from side to side. It didn't help. The bottoms of my bare feet were sore and despite not seeing any blood, I was certain they were scraped and cut.

Come, Sion bade. She started walking again. I sighed, but I followed determinedly after her. We walked for a long while and just as I started to wonder how much farther the next plateau was, I spotted a ghost waiting ahead. I quickened my pace and hoped that this final ghost was my father. When the ghost turned to face me, I stopped dead in my tracks.

It was Rory.

I remembered my conversation with Seren regarding my bond with Sion and how she said she would deal with Rory and his group. If Rory was here, then that meant she …

"Eldwin," Rory greeted. I expected anger, malice even, but he seemed happy to see me.

"Rory," I replied, but I didn't walk any closer.

"It's funny seeing you here," he said. "Since you aren't dead."

"I'm sorry. I didn't know that she was going to kill you."

"What? Who?"

"Seren," I answered.

Rory laughed. "She didn't kill me. Well, not intentionally."

"What do you mean?"

"She sent me to find her another dragon. I did find another one, but imagine my surprise when its mother swooped in and burned me to a crisp!"

My eyes widened in horror. Rory wasn't a friend, and he certainly wasn't a good person, but that didn't mean he deserved death.

"Don't look so serious about it," Rory said, still chuckling. "Being dead is so much easier. There's literally nothing to worry about."

"I suppose," I replied, still troubled.

"Listen, there are no hard feelings about what happened." Rory glanced at Sion. "You said you didn't bond with the dragon on purpose, right? I might not have believed you when I was alive, but now I know the truth. It's in the past, so forget about it."

"I can do that," I said.

"Good. Now, you'll need to fetch me a key. It should be gold. Someone called Nemryth has it."

I nodded. "Is that it?"

"Yeah, pretty much."

"Yes or no?"

"No," Rory said. "You're going to need to leave her behind." He pointed a finger at Sion. She bared her teeth at him, which looked creepy considering her form.

"I don't make the rules," he replied. "I'm just telling you."

I won't leave you behind with him, I told Sion.

She growled in response but said, *I'll be fine with him. He can't do anything to me here.*

Are you sure? If I lose you ...

You won't, Sion replied. She sounded so confident that I didn't dare doubt her.

Fine. I'll try to be back as quick as I can.

"I'm ready," I said.

Rory waved his arms around in an exaggerated

manner and a shimmering portal opened in the ground. I looked down into it, but the swirling effect made it impossible to see anything on the other side.

"Oh, one more thing," Rory said.

"What?"

"I need you to leave your sword behind, too."

"Great." I unlatched the belt around my waist and tossed the sword to Rory. It passed through his waiting hands and clattered onto the ground. I shook my head and jumped into the portal. No matter how many times I was transported by magic in this place, I doubted I would ever get used to it.

The feeling it created in my stomach was probably the worst. I tumbled end over end as multi-colored flashes of light exploded around me. Despite everything going on around me, the only thing on my mind was Maren. Sion still held my grief, but nothing could keep Maren out of my mind. Perhaps Sion had been correct. Maybe I was in love with Maren. That would certainly explain the pain I'd felt at her death.

My attention was pulled back to the present as I ceased flying through the tunnel of light. Unlike the previous two experiences, I wasn't outdoors. Instead, I found myself inside a building made of stone. It was similar to the Citadel, but the room I was in was larger than normal. At the edge of the chamber was a long table, roughly ten feet in length. Several people were seated at it, and all of them looked expectantly at me.

There was a single empty chair that I assumed was for me, so I walked over and sat down. At the head of the table sat a woman with death in her eyes. I shivered and averted my gaze from her, but everyone else was looking in her direction.

"I thought you'd never arrive," the woman said.

"Were you expecting me?" I asked.

"Of course."

"Why?"

"So that we can determine your fate."

10

"My fate?"

I looked around the table again. There were five people in total. I didn't know any of them, but I did notice that they were all wearing collars similar to Sion's. The gemstones imbedded in each collar were different, though.

"Yes, your fate," the woman at the head of the table replied. "You are charged with endangering the life of your bonded dragon, a most serious charge."

"I haven't endangered my dragon," I replied. "What are you talking about?"

The apparent leader stood from her chair and glared at me. There was an aura of power that exuded from her. The collar around her neck was silver and had black gemstones. She wasn't very tall, maybe a few inches over five feet in height. Her hair was as black as charcoal and her skin was lighter than mine.

"Shall we go over the list of transgressions?"

The others at the table muttered their agreement.

"Who are you?" I asked.

"I am Nemryth the Dark."

I silently cursed Rory's ghost for not telling me that Nemryth was going to be difficult to deal with.

She seemed to hate me already and we had just met. If she had the key I needed, this was not going to be fun.

"Forgive me," I said, "but I'm not sure what's happening."

"You have been summoned here before the Assembly to explain your crimes against your dragon," Nemryth said.

"What's the Assembly?"

"I'm growing tired of your questions," Nemryth said.

"And I'm growing tired of your attitude," I retorted. "I don't know where I am. I don't know who any of you are, and nothing has been explained to me."

For some reason, my rant made me feel a little better. It also put Nemryth off. She looked at the other members of the Assembly and they appeared to share an unspoken conversation. Nemryth looked at me and the hardness in her eyes had lessened, but they still held death.

"I apologize," Nemryth said. "It was my understanding that you knew why you were here. This is the Assembly of the Bond. We are the heads of our colors. I lead the black dragons."

"I am Brold the Eternal," the next person said. He was muscular and had short blond hair. His eyes were a piercing green hue that matched the emerald stones in his collar. "I am the head of the greens."

Risod the Tyrant, the next person spoke into my mind. She wore heavy plate armor and scars crisscrossed her face. *The red dragons call me their god.*

I looked at Nemryth questioningly.

"Risod is mute in human form," Nemryth said. "Her tongue was cut out by an enemy long ago."

I looked at the next man. His collar had sapphires. Long, straight black hair poured down past his shoulders. Aside from his hair color, he looked like the quintessential noble. His posture projected authority and his fine clothes bespoke of his wealth.

"Vandir the Great," he said. His voice was a deep baritone. He avoided looking at me, which made me smirk. He was definitely like a noble.

"Head of the blues?" I asked, guessing based on the sapphires.

Vandir tilted his head slightly in reply.

"Tyrval the Cold," the final member said. She was an elderly woman with long white hair. The gemstones in her collar were diamonds. It boggled my mind how much wealth they wore around their necks. I also found it curious that they chose to take human forms.

"I am Eldwin Baines, son of Matthias Baines," I said. "It's an honor to meet you all."

Nemryth seemed less imposing and hateful now, but she didn't take her seat.

"Now that the formalities are done, we will proceed with your crimes," she said. Nemryth laid a hand on the table and the surface shimmered with a pale blue light briefly before it was replaced with a familiar scene. It was the night Sion and I had escaped Rory's caravan. Sion was in the cart as it burned around her. The scene was frozen in place.

"After bonding with your dragon, you allowed her to be in danger of burning to death," Nemryth said.

I frowned, remembering that night much differently. "Actually, Sion put herself into that situation. She was trying to protect me and breathed fire on the cart."

"As her bonded, you should not have allowed her to risk her own life for your safety."

That logic didn't make any sense to me. I stared at Nemryth, confused.

"All here who agree with Eldwin's lack of regard, raise your hand."

All five members of the Assembly lifted their hands.

"Guilty," Nemryth said. She touched the table again and the scene changed. It showed Araphel, the fortress of the Necromancer. Sion was under a large tent eating sheep. The scene froze.

"You allowed a dragon to almost become a slave to the False King and the Necromancer," Nemryth said.

"I didn't know that's where Altin had taken me," I objected.

"Ignorance is no excuse for negligence," Brold said. "You entrusted a stranger with your dragon's life and look what happened."

"It's inexcusable," Vandir chimed in.

It was obvious I was fighting a losing battle. Yet, what did it matter? This was only some sort of twisted test to get a key. So what if they found me guilty?

"All here who agree that Eldwin was negligent?"

Again, all five members raised their hands.

Nemryth changed the image again. This time, it displayed Sion and I flying through the sky toward the dracolich. That was the night I lost my father. Again. The night Demris died.

"You rode your dragon into a battle that neither of you was ready nor trained for," Nemryth said. "And it resulted in the death of a dragon." The silence that followed her words was absolute.

"If we hadn't joined the battle, the dracolich might have taken many more lives, human and dragon alike," I said. "I regret that Demris died, but he gave his life for a worthy cause. Tell me, Assembly, where were you when the False King threatened to invade the land of the innocent?"

My words struck a nerve. Vandir clenched his jaw, but otherwise, none of them said anything.

They knew they were wrong, and that emboldened me.

"Where were you when the Necromancer raised a dragon from the dead?"

"We are not responsible for the acts of men," Brold said. "What do they with their power has nothing to do with us."

"Indeed," Vandir said. "We weren't aware of how much the Necromancer had done."

"That seems contradictory to what you just accused me of," I replied. "Didn't you say ignorance was no excuse for negligence?"

Vandir exchanged looks with Brold.

"All here who agree that Eldwin endangered his dragon a second time?"

Neemryth and Vandir raised their hands, but the other three did not.

"Not guilty," Nemryth said.

I felt some respite knowing I'd finally argued my case and won. These pompous dragons thought they were better me, just like the nobles I'd spent my life suffering under. Today was going to be different. I was going to win.

"The final crime," Nemryth said. The surface of the table shimmered and warped, revealing Sion standing with Rory. Excitement washed over me. If they thought to accuse me of leaving Sion with Rory, they were going to regret it.

"You brought your dragon to the Island of Lost

Souls for the selfish quest of finding your father."

"That's not a crime," I said.

"True, but I am not finished. You have endangered your dragon by bringing her to the path. The magic of the path has been slowly siphoning your dragon's lifeforce since she stepped on it. She's not aware of the damage yet, but when she realizes what's happening, it will be too late for her."

"I didn't know that would happen," I argued. I silently dared them to use their ignorance logic again. Surprisingly, they didn't.

"Known or not, you were warned that mortals seldom make it off the path."

"Sion chose to come with me of her own accord," I said.

"That does not negate your responsibility to ensure she is safe from danger!" Nemryth snapped. "You humans are fools! I regret the day this Assembly agreed to let our hatchlings associate with such a selfish species."

"And what of the dragons in the elven lands?" I asked. I didn't know if the elf I had spoken to had been truthful or not, but I decided to play that card. "From what I understand, they are slaves."

Nemryth looked like she could barely contain her rage. She slammed her fist onto the table and the image blinked out of existence.

"You insolent welp! What do you know?"

I shrunk backward into my chair. Her fury was intense.

"All here who agree that Eldwin is an irresponsible rider?"

Four of the members raised their hands. Tyrval was the one who refrained. She stared at me intently, but I didn't feel her in my mind.

"Guilty," Nemryth decreed. "Eldwin Baines, you are hereby stripped of your bond with Sion."

11

I gasped as searing pain ripped through me.

The bond was viciously ripped away, leaving a craterous hole inside my mind and body. All of the grief that Sion had taken away came rushing back, overwhelming my senses. I fell out of my chair and crawled on my hands and knees, trying in vain to escape. The members of the Assembly stood and watched my suffering, judgment in their eyes. Except for Tyrval. She stared at me with pity.

Like something from my imagination, but the entire room shook and the floor split open underneath me. I tumbled through the crack and fell for what felt like an eternity before I found myself at Rory's feet. I breathed in and out heavily. It was hard to imagine how I had lived before my bond with Sion. The emptiness that pervaded every part of my being was unimaginable.

"I'm sorry," Rory said. "You don't look like you got the key from Nemryth."

He helped me to my feet and looked me over.

"I don't envy you," he said. "Nemryth is …" he glanced around as if afraid she was listening. "Well, she's intense."

I managed to steady my breathing and noticed that Sion was gone. I fixed Rory with a glare of anger.

"Where is she?"

"I'm not sure," Rory replied. "She was here one moment, then the next she just disappeared."

Anger. Grief. Hated. All those emotions and more boiled within me. How could Nemryth willingly take away my bond knowing how it would make Sion feel? This island was a living nightmare. It made sense to me why the dwarf had said that few mortals made it to the end of the path. A lot of things made sense now.

"Don't forget your sword," Rory said, trying to nudge the hilt with his boot. His ghostly outline passed through it.

"Don't leave," I begged softly. As much as I didn't care for Rory, I didn't want to be alone.

"I can't stay, Eldwin. My time here is done."

I looked up and he was gone. I had never felt more alone in my entire life, not even after my mother had passed away from her sickness. There was something whole, something fulfilling that the bond brought with it. I laid on the stones of the path and wept, my sobs wracking my entire body. I couldn't go any further. I'd lost everything dear to me and gained nothing.

"I give up," I whispered.

The sound of someone approaching from behind me caught my attention, but I didn't bother to look. The steps paused momentarily, then the person walked around me and came into view. It was Master Pevus.

"Eldwin," he said gently. "You must keep going. Time is running short."

"I don't want to," I choked. "I just want to stay right here until the end."

Master Pevus sat down on the path and remained silent. A long while passed before he spoke again. "This path has taught me many things. Patience, strength, resilience. What has it taught you?"

"Nothing," I said.

"Nothing at all? That seems like quite a waste of time and energy. You've been through a lot, and yet you've learned nothing from it all? What of your first plateau?"

"I walked across hardened lava to get a key. I'd hardly say that taught me anything."

"Yes, but you walked across it barefoot."

"And?" I said.

"Did you burn your feet?"

"Yes."

"Then you know that you're not invincible. Your true strength against obstacles comes from within. You can push your limits, but everyone has to learn where those limits are."

I laughed. That's what he expected me to learn from that? I didn't get that connection at all.

"How about losing Maren?"

"Don't remind me," I said.

"You didn't learn that the fate of those around you is often in your hands?"

"No, actually. If I learned anything, it's that this island is a giant torture chamber for the sadistic pleasure of some powerful wizard or god."

"Come now, Eldwin," Master Pevus admonished. "You're blinding yourself to what the path was trying to teach you."

"Which is what?"

Master Pevus sighed. "I cannot tell you what you have learned. The path demands much—"

"—and returns little," I said, cutting him off. "Yeah, I got it."

"Yet what the path returns is of immeasurable value."

The ground rumbled beneath me, reminding me of the impending eruption. Perhaps that was what I needed. To become a ghost. At least then I would be with my parents *and* Maren.

"Walk with me," Pevus said, standing. He offered me his hand.

"No," I replied.

"Just up the hill. It'll be worth it."

I considered telling him to leave me alone, but what more did I have to lose? I forced myself to my feet, ignoring his help.

"Fine," I said.

Master Pevus smiled and started walking. I

followed behind him, wiping my face on my sleeve. My clothes were likely dirtier than me, but I didn't care. We didn't walk far when I saw that the path ended at the entrance of a cave. I stopped walking.

"I'm not submitting myself for more torture," I said.

"There are no more trials," Master Pevus replied. "This is the Cave of Reward."

I wanted to be stubborn, but I found myself walking closer. Whispering voices were coming from the cave. They were soothing and produced feelings of peace. I looked over my shoulder at Master Pevus and he motioned for me to continue. He'd never steered me wrong before, so I turned my gaze ahead and entered the darkness of the cave.

I walked slowly and kept my hands outstretched in front of me so that I didn't bump into anything. A brilliant light suddenly illuminated the darkness and blinded me. I blocked the light with my hands, but it was so bright that it shined through my flesh, exposing my bones and veins.

"You have reached the end of this journey," a disembodied voice said. "Step forth and receive your reward."

The light dimmed and as my eyes adjusted, I became aware that I was no longer alone. I could feel the bond with Sion again. Her excitement and joy flooded into my mind and I laughed and rushed forward to embrace her. Tears streamed freely down my face.

"I thought I'd lost you forever," I whispered.

The path had other plans, Sion replied.

Behind Sion, I saw Maren. I released Sion and before I could wrap my arms around Maren, she tackled me. We fell onto the ground and she hugged me tightly. She pressed her warm lips against my cheek.

"I knew you would make it to the end," Maren said.

"That makes one of us," I replied. "I gave up out there, Maren. I was ready to—"

"Don't say it," she said, placing a finger against my lips. "Don't."

I nodded. She untangled herself from me and we got up. I spotted my boots and put them on.

"How do we get out of here?" I asked.

Maren shrugged and Sion looked around the cave. The way I had come in was mysteriously closed. A scraping sound filled the chamber and I saw a natural doorway had opened ahead. We walked together, Sion and Maren on either side of me. Maren grabbed my mangled hand and squeezed it.

We stepped through the threshold and there were two figures partially hidden behind tall pillars.

"Demris!" Maren shouted excitedly. She ran forward, almost jerking my arm out of its socket, and headed for the figure on the right. I didn't recognize him in human form, but I did recognize the other figure.

It was my father.

"Eldwin, is that you?"

I rushed to him and attempted to embrace him, but my arms passed through his form. I felt stupid for a moment, but my father smiled and everything else fell away from my mind.

"Father … I've finally found you!"

"It's so great to you see you, son. But … what are you doing here?" he asked. "*How* did you get here?"

"I paid the ferryman to bring me," I replied. "And I came here to find you."

"How did you know I would be here?"

"I didn't," I said. "It was a risk, but it paid off. I can't believe I found you!" I was ecstatic. Finally, after everything I'd endured up the path, I had found my father's soul. The ground shuddered and I grabbed onto the pillar to steady myself. The tremors were getting stronger.

"We need to hurry," I said. "The volcano is about to go off, and we need to get back to the coast. The ferryman will take us back to the mainland."

"Eldwin, slow down. What are you going on about?"

"I've come to bring you back to the land of the living," I said.

My father frowned and pursed his lips.

"What is it?" I asked.

"I'm sorry, Eldwin. I'm not going back."

12

"What?" I was dumbstruck. "What do you mean you can't come back?"

"It's not that I can't," my father said. "It's that I won't."

That couldn't be what he said. I had to be hearing things.

"I don't understand," I said. "I came all this way … I've been through the toughest time of my life."

"Please don't mistake my words. It's not that I don't want to be with you. Try to see it from my perspective. I died ten years ago, then I was magically enslaved back into a body and forced to serve the Necromancer. I want peace, Eldwin. And I've found peace by not being tethered to the world and its pain."

That made sense. I couldn't fault him for wanting to have rest, and I certainly had never considered that he wouldn't want to come back with me. Perhaps I had been selfish with my decision and hadn't realized it.

"I'm sorry. I just assumed and … I shouldn't have."

"You have nothing to apologize for," my father said. "You've grown into a great man, Eldwin. I'm proud of you and it gives my heart joy to see that you've bonded so strongly with your dragon."

My heart swelled with pride at his words and my emotions overcame me. I hadn't cried this much for as long as I could remember.

"You keep good company," my father added, nodding toward Maren.

"She has a good heart, but she can be rebellious," I replied with a smile.

"The best women are," he laughed.

"If you won't come back with us, then I feel like this journey was fruitless."

"How so?" My father asked.

"The whole reason I came here was to find you."

"I can tell by their interaction that her dragon's death was not a natural one. What happened?" He asked.

"Demris was killed by the dracolich," I replied. "She's been heartbroken ever since. In my last test or whatever that was, my bond was revoked by the Assembly. I can understand her pain now."

"You saw the Assembly?"

I couldn't tell if my father's surprise was good or bad.

"I did."

"Interesting," he said. He watched Maren and Demris for a moment, then looked at me and lowered his voice. "You know dragons can cross back into the world of the living, right?"

I nodded. "Master Pevus mentioned that all souls could," I replied.

My father smiled knowingly and I realized what he was hinting at.

"I know what I must do," I said. "I'm going to miss you. More than before, now that I've had time with you."

"I've missed you and your mother since I died. Now I will be with her again, but your time is not up yet. With the Conclave gone, there will be a need for leaders like you and your friend. Go and make the world a better place."

"I will try," I said.

"That is all anyone can ask for," my father replied. He looked up for a moment and his ghostly form seemed to fade slightly. "My time here is over. I love you, Eldwin. Never forget that."

And then he was gone. I stood there quietly for a while, imagining my father still standing there. We'd lost so much time together, but the few moments I'd just had with him were invaluable. I wiped my eyes with the sleeve of my shirt and turned my attention to Maren. She looked so happy.

I joined them and cleared my throat. Maren looked at me, a wide grin stretched across her lips. She glanced behind me and her face scrunched in confusion.

"Where's your father?" She asked.

"He's gone," I answered. "His purpose was

fulfilled."

"I'm sorry, Eldwin," Maren said sadly. "I know how much you wanted him back."

"It's all right, I guess. It'll take some time to work through everything, but I'll be fine. This journey wasn't wasted, though. You found Demris, and that's worth every trial I faced."

"Thank you," she replied. Her eyes watered and she blinked rapidly to clear the tears away.

"We need to get back to the coast. There's just one problem."

"What?"

"We don't have a body for Demris," I said.

"I've been thinking about that," Maren replied. "I haven't come up with a solution."

"Neither have I."

I can help, Sion said.

How? I asked, turning to face her.

I can let Demris's soul temporarily reside in my body with me. I've never done it before, but I heard of a dragon doing it once when I was with Rory. I don't know how long I'll be able to keep his soul within me, but I'll do what I can.

Are you sure? I asked.

Yes. Demris would do the same for me.

"Sion says she'll help. Demris can join her inside her body, but she doesn't know how long she'll be able to hold him."

"Thank you," Maren said to Sion. "I am indebted to you. Name anything you want and you shall have it."

That's not necessary, Sion told me.

"Sion says don't worry about it," I said. "Once we get to the mainland, then what? Sion might be able to temporarily hold him, but he's going to need a body of his own."

"His body was taken to the Citadel," Maren replied.

"I'm sure they've burned his remains by now," I said.

"No. I …" Maren looked down at the ground sheepishly. "I cast a preserving spell on his body. I didn't think I'd ever see him again, but I thought I could keep his memory longer if I could spend time with him in some way."

"Well, it sounds like your idea turned out for the best. I think we can wait until we get on the boat for them to share her body. The less time she has to hold him, the higher the chances are we can make this work."

The ground trembled again and I exchanged looks with Maren.

"Any idea how we can get out of here?" I asked.

There, Sion said. She pointed across the chamber to the far wall. There was a portal that rippled in the air. I led the way and stepped through it. Unlike the other portals, this one didn't make my stomach flip. I was standing at the beginning of the path, looking out at the ghostly armies that were still battling each other.

My companions appeared beside me and we continued across the field. I couldn't quite remember the exact way we'd come, but I tried to keep the path directly behind us. Before long, I could hear the sound of the waves crashing against the shore.

"We're almost there," I announced.

Maren hadn't talked much, but I assumed it was because she was communicating with Demris. I really hoped our plan would work. It would be heartbreaking to see Maren lose Demris again. We reached the coast but I didn't see the ferryman. The ground trembled again, stronger this time, and I was worried we weren't going to make it off the island in time.

"Where's the ferryman?" Maren asked.

"I don't see him," I replied. I started jogging, scanning the shoreline for a sign of the old man.

Over there, Sion said. *He's coming through the fog.*

I stopped at the edge of the water and waited. A dark outline formed in the fog, then the boat and the ferryman broke free of the thick haze. The boat slid onto the sandy shore and a host of souls disembarked. The ferryman saw us and waved us forward.

"I have to be honest," he said. "I didn't expect to see any of you again."

"Thanks for the confidence," I replied. "If you didn't think we'd make it, why did you make a deal with Maren?"

"It was a risk, true, but I couldn't resist the opportunity."

"Have you decided what you want?" Maren asked.

"Yes, I think I have, but I won't tell you just yet."

What do you need to do to allow Demris into your body? I asked Sion.

I'm not sure. Give me a moment to figure it out.

A thunderous cracking sound echoed through the air and I watched in fascinated horror as the top of the volcano exploded.

"Hurry!" I shouted aloud, not bothering to speak through the bond.

Sion closed her eyes. I waited, but nothing was happening. As I was about to say something, Sion opened her mouth and began to inhale Demris's soul. His ghostly body slowly faded from sight, and once he was completely gone, Sion opened her eyes.

This is more difficult than I thought, she said. *Tell the ferryman to go as fast as he can.*

"Let's go," I said, pushing Maren into the boat. Sion climbed in and I followed after them. "We need you to get us back as quickly as possible," I said to the ferryman.

"This journey takes time," he replied. "I don't control the speed, just the direction."

"Just do what you can, will you?"

The old man shrugged his thin shoulders and pushed off the shore. The boat glided over the water and seemed to take an eternity to leave the island behind.

"Are we in danger of the eruption?" I asked.

"No," the ferryman answered. "It blows off steam sometimes, but nothing ever travels past the island's borders."

I didn't believe him, but as we continued across the sea and nothing bad happened, I decided maybe he knew what he was talking about.

"About my boon," he said.

"Yes?" Maren asked. "What would you like?"

"I want you to take my place on the ferry."

13

"Absolutely not," I said, glaring at the old man.

"He's right," Maren chimed in. "I can't do that."

"I didn't say it was permanent. I only want three days to go ashore. It's been a very long time since I've seen another person. Meeting you has made me homesick."

"No," I replied, shaking my head.

Maren looked at me and I could see the rebelliousness in her eyes. I tried to make myself look stern, but Maren rolled her eyes.

"I can do that," she said. "Three days and you'll be back. Promise?"

"On my life," the ferryman said.

I didn't like their arrangement. At all. Yet I knew that once Maren made her mind up about something, it was impossible to stop her. I sighed and moved to the back of the boat and stared off into the fog. I supposed three days wasn't the end of the world, but we had to get Demris's soul back to his body quickly and the boat seemed to barely be moving.

"Can't this thing go any faster?" I complained.

"Patience, boy," the ferryman replied. "She has a steady pace."

I rolled my eyes and continued to watch the fog.

We drifted lazily across the sea and I grew bored and annoyed. After a while, I noticed that anxiety was flooding the bond between Sion and myself. I turned to look at her. She was standing near the front of the boat, ahead of the ferryman, and she was wringing her hands together.

Are you all right? I asked.

It's Demris, Sion replied. *I'm not sure, but I think something is wrong.*

What do you mean?

He feels ... strange. Different. He's struggling to get out of my body.

Try to keep him in as long as you can, I said.

I'm trying, but his strength is formidable.

"Maren." I motioned for her.

She came and sat beside me. "You're mad at me, I know."

"No, I'm not," I replied.

"Yes, you are. You've been sulking over here ever since I agreed to his offer."

"I'm not sulking, I'm ... never mind. Sion says Demris is trying to get out."

Maren turned her attention to Sion. "I can't feel the bond, so I don't think I can communicate with him," she said. "I can try, though."

She closed her eyes. I looked from her to Sion and back, over and over, until Maren opened her eyes.

"I don't feel him at all," she said. "I tried to communicate to him through Sion, but she's not my dragon. I'm not sure how to reach him."

"Here," I offered my hand. "See if you can feel him through my bond with Sion."

"I don't think that'll work," Maren replied.

"It doesn't hurt to try," I said.

"True."

Maren grabbed onto my hand and I closed my eyes and pictured the bond, then tried to picture Maren as a globe of light. As she spoke, the globe flashed brightly and sent tendrils of smoke to the bond. I couldn't hear the words, not audibly, but I could *feel* them.

Demris! Please hold on. We're trying to get you back!

Exhaustion overwhelmed me and the connection between us all broke. I opened my eyes and slumped against Maren, feeling unsteady.

"Are you going to pass out?" She asked.

"I'm not sure," I replied. I remained still and eventually felt my strength return, but the tiredness persisted. "I think I'm all right now."

I sat up straight and blinked a few times. My vision blurred and everything was distorted. I could see the gemstones of Sion's collar glowing and tried to keep my focus on them. After a moment of intense nausea, everything returned to normal.

"That was weird," I said. "Is Demris still trying

to get out?"

No, Sion replied. Her voice was strained.

Are you sure?

Yes! She snapped.

I looked at the ferryman. "I know this thing moves at its own pace, but we really need to get to shore."

The ferryman glowered at me. "I told you—"

Whatever he said was drowned out by a deafening cry. Sion's face turned bright red as she roared. The glow of the gemstones intensified, becoming blindingly bright. I had to turn away, but as I did, I thought I saw green smoke snake out of Sion's parted lips.

The boat shook and I grabbed onto Maren. The ferryman shouted something and then the boat overturned. Suddenly, I was underwater. Despite the sunlight, I couldn't tell which way was up and I began to panic as the water got up my nostrils. I tried not to cough, but the air forced its way out and I began choking.

Something strong wrapped around my chest and then my head broke the surface of the water. I coughed again, spitting out the nasty tasting seawater. I tried to see who had helped me, but I couldn't turn my neck far enough. I saw the capsized boat floating a few feet away, but there was no sign of Maren or Sion.

"Blasted dragon," the ferryman cursed and I

realized who was pulling me.

My feet touched the bottom and the ferryman released me from his grip. I turned around and the two of us headed for the shore. I was relieved to see Maren and Sion not far away, wading through the water. They reached the beach before we did and waited for us.

"What happened?" I asked.

Demris fled my body, Sion replied.

Do you sense him nearby?

Yes. We need to leave. She sounded worried and I thought it best not to question her.

"Let's go," I said to Maren.

"What about my boat?" The ferryman asked. "This is your fault. You need to help me retrieve it."

"We can come back for it later," I said. "I think we're in danger right now."

"What do you mean?" Maren asked. "What's going on?"

"Demris got out," I said. "Sion's afraid, which means we need to go. Now!"

The ferryman started to object, but his words became garbled and he fell to his knees, his hands clasping at his throat. I backed away in terror. The ferryman struggled to breathe, his face turning red like Sion's had, then his struggling ceased and his arms fell uselessly at his sides. The old man collapsed into the sand.

Green smoke escaped the ferryman's mouth and drifted into the air. Sion took a step toward the smoke, but it ascended higher and flew away from her, heading inland. We stood wordlessly, staring after Demris's soul.

"We have to find him," Maren said.

"Yeah, before he kills anyone else," I replied.

"He didn't do that intentionally."

"How do you know that?" I asked.

"Because Demris isn't like that!" Maren snapped.

Master Pevus's words echoed in the back of my mind. "He may not be the dragon you remember. Master Pevus said souls don't always come back the same. Something might have happened to him."

Maren glared at me, but I could see the fear in her eyes. She knew I was right. I didn't say anything else because I didn't want to hurt her. She'd lost Demris once, and now she may have just lost him again.

This was supposed to work. We were supposed to have Demris back, but everything just turned into more of a nightmare than the island had been.

Can you track him? I asked Sion.

If he doesn't get too far, she replied.

Then we need to hurry.

I walked over to Sion and unclasped the collar. It fell into the sand at Sion's feet and for a moment, nothing happened. Then slowly her body began to grow and change colors. Her human appearance twisted and altered until her dragon form was complete. She stretched her legs and flexed her wings.

"We'll find him," I said to Maren. "I promise."

"Don't make promises you can't keep," she replied, then climbed up Sion's shoulder and onto her back. I cast a final glance at the dead ferryman and shook my head sadly.

"That poor man," I whispered. Who would ferry the wayward souls to the island now? I shrugged the thought away and grabbed the collar from the sand, then climbed onto Sion's back. She flapped her wings and lifted off the ground, then followed in the direction Demris had gone. The scenery was a blur as I stared ahead looking for green smoke. One thing kept repeating in my mind.

What had we done?

THE END OF BOOK FOUR

ABOUT THE AUTHOR

Richard Fierce is a fantasy and space opera author. He's been writing since childhood, but began publishing in 2007. Since then, he's written multiple novels and short stories.

In 2000, Richard won Poet of the Year for his poem *The Darkness*. He's also one of the creative brains behind the Allatoona Book Festival, a literary event in Acworth, Georgia.

A recovering retail worker, he now works in the tech industry when he's not busy writing.

He's married and has three step-daughters (pray for him), three dogs (two huskies!), three cats, two ferrets and a fish. He basically has a zoo.

His love affair with fantasy was born in high school when a friend's mother gave him a copy of *Dragons of Spring Dawning* by Margaret Weis and Tracy Hickman.

www.ingramcontent.com/pod-product-compliance
Lightning Source LLC
Chambersburg PA
CBHW032039180726
48284CB00008B/2664